INSIGHT PUBLICA

Kozhikode, Kerala, India
www.insightpublica.com
e-mail: insightpublica@gmail.com
Title: Style and the Man
Author: Meredith Nicholson
(English)
First Insight Publica Edition: October 2021
Copyright©Reserved

ISBN 978-93-5517-141-2

STYLE AND THE MAN
Meredith Nicholson

Nicholson was born on December 9, 1866, in Crawfordsville, Indiana, to Edward Willis Nicholson and the former Emily Meredith. Largely self-taught, Nicholson began a newspaper career in 1884 at the Indianapolis Sentinel. He moved to the Indianapolis News the following year, where he remained until 1897.

He wrote Short Flights in 1891, and continued to publish extensively, both poetry and prose until 1928. During the first quarter of the 20th century, Nicholson, along with Booth Tarkington, George Ade, and James Whitcomb Riley helped to create a Golden Age of literature in Indiana. Three of his books from that era were national bestsellers: The House of a Thousand Candles (#4 in 1906), The Port of Missing Men (#3 in 1907), and A Hoosier Chronicle (#5 in 1912).

In 1928, Nicholson entered Democratic party politics, and served for two years as a city councilman in Indianapolis. He rose through the ranks of the Democratic party and was rewarded with appointments as Envoy to Paraguay, Venezuela, and Nicaragua.

Nicholson was married first to Eugenie Clementine Kountze, daughter of Herman Kountze, and then to Dorothy Wolfe Lannon, whom he later divorced.

Nicholson died on December 21, 1947, in Indianapolis, aged 81, and is buried in the Crown Hill Cemetery.

STYLE AND THE MAN

AT the word style the critics at once sit up and take notice. We are all sensitive to style; we either like to drift with an easy, lazy current, or we prefer to fight a turbulent, resisting tide; we enjoy contemplating the moonlight upon tranquil waters, or we find our greatest pleasure in watching the ruffian billows breaking against rough shores. These are largely matters of temperament or of mood. The attitude of many of us changes from day to day, from book to book; but at heart we all have a preference, a prejudice in favor of certain methods of writing, while others awake our antagonism. It has probably been the experience of all of us that books that reach the library table often lie unopened for many days; and then to our own surprise we some day take them up, read them with delight, and wonder why we approached them so reluctantly. In the same whimsical fashion we recur to volumes that we knew in old times, impelled by some instinct that makes us long to experience the same emotion, the same thrill, the same peace that gladdened our souls in happier days. There are books that fit into moods of sorrow, of loneliness, of anxiety; and others are equally identified with moods of happiness, elation and hope. There are in all our libraries, great or small, stern Gibraltars that rise gloomily before us on shelves to which we never turn with pleasure.

Great writers have rarely written of style, perhaps because it is so individual, so intimate a matter; and the trick of the thing may not, except in rare cases be communicated to the tyro. The convenient methods of absent treatment advertised by correspondence schools of authorship are of no avail in the business of style; style can no more be taught than the shadows of clouds across June meadows, or the play of wind over wheat fields can be directed or influenced by the hand of man. To grasp style much is inevitably presupposed,—grammar, sensibility, taste, a feeling for color and rhythm,—of such things as these is the kingdom of style. In children we often observe an individual and distinctive way of saying things; we all have correspondents whose letters are a joy because of their vivid revelation of the writer. In every community there are persons much quoted for their wit or wisdom, whose sayings have a raciness and tang.

The bulk of English is so enormous and increases so rapidly that we have a right to pick and choose and to hang aloof from all that does not please us. The fashion changes in literary style as in clothes, and yet,—to shift the figure,—the snows of yesteryear linger on the far uplands and high peaks, and they are there forever. It is a common impression that popular taste in literature is bad and growing worse. I do not myself sympathize with this idea. The complaint smells of antiquity: every age has had its literary Jeremiahs; the wail that of making many books there is no end is older than American literature; for is it not written: "Many of them also which used curious arts brought their books together and burned them before all men; and they counted the price of them and found it fifty thousand pieces of silver."

It would be instructive, if there were time, to review the labors of those who have first and last written on the subject of style. We might with profit and entertainment discuss the general superiority of English poetry to English prose; but this is a matter conceded, I believe, by sounder critics than your orator; we might linger by the golden coasts of Greece and harken to the voice of Plato who—says Frederic Harrison, alone is faultless; we might follow Cæsar's eagles into Roman territory and hear, at the Sabine farm, Ars Poetica read by a most competent witness on this question of style. Here is a man to our liking, this Horace, and we find him eminently modern in his attitude toward the dictionary: "Mortal works must perish," he says, who was born two thousand years ago; "much less can the honor and elegance of language be long-lived. Many words shall revive which now have fallen off; and many words which are now in esteem shall fall off, if it be the will of custom, in whose power is the decision and right and standard of language." Other witnesses speaking many tongues crowd the door, but we must stick to our text. It is our mother English that now concerns us, and only a few may be allowed to testify at this session of the court. You will not, I pray, take my obiter dicta too seriously. I beg you to deal leniently with my stupidity when I say that such prose as Addison's or Steele's has little charm for me; it is, as Mr. James might say, nice; but it lacks variety, flash, ginger; and if I prefer Swift, Defoe or Carlyle to Milton, pray do not deliver me to the lions. As an advocate of the open shop in criticism I insist on my right to punch and hammer at my own bench in the corner beside yours. In thus frankly divulging my likings and aversions, I hope—to quote Doctor Johnson, that "I am not preparing for my future life either shame or repentance." Let us assume that all the authoritative testimony on this subject is in evidence and a part of the res gestæ,—Newman on Language in "The Idea of a University"; Spencer's

"Philosophy of Style"; certain passages from George Henry Lewes' "Principles of Success in Literature"; De Quincey's eloquent and stimulating essay on "Style"; and discussions of the same fascinating subject by Stevenson, Pater and Frederic Harrison, and by Antoine Albalat in French,—these we file with the clerk. And not to know Professor Walter Raleigh's essay on Style is to have missed a discussion of the subject which is in itself a model of graceful, melodious writing, guiltless of preciosity.

There must always be a difference between the style of genius and that which proceeds from ordered, controlled and directed talent. The dead level of mediocrity is easily attained in both prose and poetry, but even persons of little cultivation feel the lure of captivating speech. The world has been swayed by the power of phrase. The trumpet and drum may take hold of man's emotions, but words only can touch his mind with truth. The words of Jesus are marvelously simple; there were undoubtedly those among his contemporaries who could contrive more splendid orations; there were citizens of the Roman empire of which he was a humble citizen who were richer in learning.

Antoine Albalat, in "The Travail of Style," discusses in separate chapters the literary methods of such writers of supreme rank as Pascal, Bossuet, Buffon, Montesquieu, Rousseau, La Fontaine, Racine, Balzac,

Chateaubriand, Victor Hugo and Flaubert. And he conducts this discussion in an immensely interesting and original way, namely, by reproducing the actual manuscripts of the great writers themselves, with the countless erasures and substitutions of words, phrases and whole passages they made. What toilers, what galley slaves of the pen, they were! one cries in amazement! The first draught is as nothing. It serves simply as a point of departure, to blot, to cover with spider tracks of erasures and emendations.

"Is this the work of inspiration, this galley-slave toil at the dull mechanic pen?" demands a critic. "Yes," the writer of the book replies. "When Buffon declared 'Genius is but infinite capacity of patience,' do you take him for a fool who meant to say: 'If the veriest dolt sits long enough on a chalk egg he will hatch out a phoenix'? No, he meant that as much inspiration of genius goes into thoughtful correction and brooding revision as into the first jet of composition. When the now more fiery, more pathetic word suggests itself, it is even more a flash of inspiration than the primary suggestion of the older and poorer one." Ah! if ever there was a book to confirm the current saying, "Easy writing makes hard reading," it is this.

There is, as every one knows, an apparent happy luck in writing,—the curiosa felicitas that puts the inevitable word into your ink pot. I offer the suggestion that composition does not begin with the taking up of the pen; that there are untraceable sub-conscious processes that are never idle, whose results illuminate many a treasured book. He were a rash author who would attempt to set apart his conscious felicities from his inadvertent graces. How long do you suppose Shakespeare pondered that most stupendous incident in all literature—the knocking at the gate in Macbeth? Tennyson when questioned as to his own power over words once solemnly answered: "In the beginning was the word, and the word was with God and the word was God"—implying a belief in inspiration.

Veracity is the final test in all art. It makes no difference how trifling or unimportant the thing that we would utter, or whether we express ourselves in the cadences of the symphony, in the militant splendor of the epic, in the careless fling of some vagrant poet's tavern catch; or whether the artist writes a landscape in colors upon canvas, the test of beauty and strength is first of all the test of truth. We measure the far-shadowing spear of Achilles and weigh the gleaming sword of Arthur by the things we know to be beautiful and strong. Words may lie before us like green meadows by peaceful streams, but we must feel the softness of the turf and hear the bubble of the stream or they fail as a vehicle; or, in other departments of literature, they must sweep toward us like a cavalry charge, and we must hear the rattle of scabbards and the pounding of hoofs until we draw back struck with fear at the onset, or the artist, who is like a captain over his troop, has failed of his purpose. "My love for thee," wrote the poet; "my love for thee shall march like armed men."

The power of the printed word has always been tremendous; the authority of type is often excessive and unjustified; yet this only makes more exacting the inevitable standard of truth. Style will forever be challenged by truth, that austere higher critic whose method is so searching and whose judgments are so inexorable. The mere bows and ruffles, the chiffon flounces of composition are easily flung off by the literary milliner, but unless they are essential to the investiture of character they crumple and pass to the garret. It is not enough to communicate to the eye the sense of form, the outward and visible outline of a man; the shop keeper can do that with a dummy in his show-window; but words must go further and produce bone and sinew; we must be able through the writer's magic to clasp a hand that is quick with red blood; whose contact thrills us at a touch.

This is as true in those characterizations that are the veritable creatures of realism as of those that are wrought in the mood of romance. The burden upon your romancer lies, in fact, more heavily, for in his work the spectator, the auditor, the reader, can assist him little. Silas Lapham, for example, is within the range of our common experience; what the author may omit we supply; whereas D'Artagnan rides in from a strange and unexplored land, and we must be convinced of his cleverness, his courage, his skill with the sword. When Beatrix comes down the stair to meet Esmond we must hear the rustle of her skirts, feel the fascination of her smile, and be won by the charm of her voice;—we must hear the pretty click of her slippers on the stairs. And we may say, in passing, that Thackeray carried style as an element of English fiction higher than it was ever carried before and no one since has shaken his supremacy.

Few writers of the Victorian period wielded a more flexible English than Matthew Arnold, and few writers of any period have shown greater versatility. His power of direct statement was very great and he plunged forward to the chief facts he wished to present with the true journalist's instinct for what is interesting and important. As a controversial writer he had few equals in his day, and many philistines went down before his lance. The force of repetition was never more effectively illustrated than in the letters he launched against his assailants. He was a master of irony, and irony in skilled hands is a terrible weapon.

The vivacious Mr. Birrell complains of the jauntiness of Arnold's style in "Literature and Dogma," and we must confess that Arnold pinned his tick-tack on the palace windows of the bishops of Gloucester and Winchester rather too often. But Arnold had, too, the touch of grace and melody. He was a master of the mournful cadence, as witness the familiar and oft quoted paragraph on Newman at Saint Mary's with which he opens his lecture on Emerson; and even more beautiful is that passage in one of the most appealing and charming of his literary essays—the paper on Keats—in which he thus plays upon Keats' own words: "By virtue of his feeling for beauty and of his perception of the vital connection of beauty with truth, Keats accomplished so much in poetry, than in one of the two great modes by which poetry interprets, in the faculty of naturalistic interpretation, in what we call natural magic, he ranks with Shakespeare. 'The tongue of Kean,' he says, in an admirable criticism of that great actor and his enchanting elocution; 'the tongue of Kean must seem to have robbed the Hybla bees and left them honeyless. There is an indescribable gusto in his voice;—in Richard, "Be stirring with the lark to-morrow, gentle Norfolk!" comes from him as through the morning atmosphere towards which he yearns.' This magic," says Arnold, "this 'indescribable gusto in the voice,' Keats himself, too, exhibits in his poetic expression. No one else in English poetry, save Shakespeare, has in expression quite the fascinating felicity of Keats, his perfection of loveliness. 'I think,' he said humbly, 'I shall be among the English poets after my death.' He is; he is with Shakespeare."

The great distinction of Newman's style lies in its extraordinary clarity. He wrote for a select audience; his sermons even were for the scholars of his university, and dealt usually with the fine points of religious philosophy. He was under scrutiny, the chief spokesman of one of the most remarkable movements that ever shook the Protestant world, and of necessity he expressed himself with scrupulous precision. After crystal clearness a certain cloistral composure follows naturally as a second characteristic of his style. He was engaged upon a serious business and never trifled with it. It is unfortunate for literature that he confined himself so closely to theological controversy or to kindred subjects that have lost their hold on popular interest, for in the qualities indicated—clearness and precision, and in melody—he is rarely equaled in the whole range of English prose. Religion in his case was not a matter of emotion but of intellect. Personal feeling flashes out so rarely in his pages that we hover with attention over those few lines in which he tells us of his good-by to Oxford, and of his farewell to Trinity College: "Trinity, which was so dear to me, and which held on its foundation so many who had been kind to me both when I was a boy, and all through my Oxford life. Trinity had never been unkind to me. There used to be much snap-dragon growing on the walls opposite my freshman's rooms there, and I had for years taken it as the emblem of my own perpetual residence even unto death in my University."

But there for a moment he was off guard: and for an instance of his more characteristic manner—for an example of that mournful music which Arnold, in the familiar paragraph to which I have referred, caught so happily,—we do better to dip into such a sermon as the famous one on The Theory of Development, and I read from the page as it falls open:

"Critical disquisitions are often written about the idea which this or that poet might have in his mind in certain of his compositions and characters: and we call such analysis the philosophy of poetry, not implying thereby of necessity that the author wrote upon such a theory in his actual delineation, or knew what he was doing; but that, in matter of fact, he was possessed, ruled, guided by an unconscious idea. Moreover, it is a question whether that strange and painful feeling of unreality which religious men experience from time to time, when nothing seems true, or good, or right, or profitable, when faith seems a name, and duty a mockery, and all endeavors to do right, absurd and hopeless, and all things forlorn and dreary, as if religion were wiped out from the world, may not be the direct effect of the temporary obscuration of some master vision, which unconsciously supplies the mind with spiritual life and peace."

Here in America style was first greatly realized by Hawthorne. Changing tastes and fashions have not shaken his position. He was our first, and he remains our greatest creative artist in fiction, and it were idle to dispute his position. His work became classic almost in his own day. He was no chance adventurer upon the sea of literature, but a deliberate, painstaking artist. Fiction has rarely been served by so noble a spirit; and fortunate were we indeed could we pluck the secret of style from his pages. In his narrative there may sometimes be dull passages; his instinct for form and proportion may seem at times, by our later tastes, to fail him; but his command of the language is never lost; his apt choice of words moves an imitator to despair; and felicity of phrase, balance, movement and color were greatly his. The cumulative power of "The Scarlet Letter" is tremendous,—and it is a power of style not less than of intense moral earnestness. There is something awe-inspiring in the contemplation of that melancholy figure, in whose mind and heart the spirit of Puritanism dwelt as in a sanctuary; and yet he was always and above everything else an artist. He was as incapable of an inartistic idea as he was of a clumsy sentence. Sitting at the receipt of custom in the grim little village of Salem he took toll of stranger ships than ever touched Salem wharves. Other figures in American literature must be scrutinized through the magnifying glass; Hawthorne alone looms huge;—as Mr. James so happily said of Balzac, Hawthorne's figure is immovable and fixed for all time. To mention Irving, Poe or Cooper on the same page is but to betray our incompetence for the office of criticism. There are kindlier and cheerfuller figures among American prose writers, but Hawthorne alone is commanding, noble, august.

After Hawthorne, the prose of Lowell affords, I should say, the highest mark reached by any American writer. The main difference,—and it is a difference of height, breadth, depth,—the difference between them as prose writers lies in the fact that one was a creative artist and the other a critic. And criticism must always be secondary. The enduring monuments of the literature of all the ages were built before criticism was born. The great originals in all literature have paid little heed to criticism. The creator must plow and sow and reap; the critic may only seek the garnered harvest, nibble the hay and chew his cud. The persistent efforts of critics to magnify their own importance proves their sensitiveness and the jealousy with which they guard their self-conferred prerogatives. The criticism of literature is the only business in which the witness is not called upon to qualify as to his competency. Failures at any game naturally turn critic. In science we demand the critic's credentials: in literature we all kick the sleeping lion and inadvertently twist his tail.

Lowell wrote with remarkable knowledge, skill and effectiveness on many subjects, and his political and literary essays are models of form and diction. He was perhaps the most cultivated man we have produced; he drew from all literatures, and not less from human experience; and he was singular among American scholars in his life-long attention to politics. He saw American history in the making through years of great civil and military stress. He was one of the first to take the true measure of Lincoln. He wrote a magnificent prose essay on Lincoln before our martyred chief passed to the shadows; and the postscript to that essay touches, it seems to me, the higher altitudes possible in prose, and deserves to be remembered and repeated side by side with his Commemoration Ode:

"On the day of his death this simple Western attorney, who, according to one party was a vulgar joker, and whom the doctrinaires among his own supporters accused of wanting every element of statesmanship, was the most absolute ruler in Christendom, and this solely by the hold his good-humored sagacity had laid on the hearts and understandings of his countrymen. Nor was this all, for it appeared that he had drawn the great majority, not only of his fellow-citizens, but of mankind also, to his side. So strong and so persuasive is honest manliness without a single quality of romance or unreal sentiment to help it! A civilian during times of the most captivating military achievement; awkward, with no skill in the lower technicalities of manners, he left behind him a fame beyond that of any conqueror, the memory of a grace higher than that of outward person, and of a gentlemanliness deeper than mere breeding. Never before that startled April morning did such multitude of men shed tears for the death of one they had never seen, as if with him a friendly presence had been taken away from their lives, leaving them colder and darker. Never was funeral panegyric so eloquent as the silent look of sympathy which strangers exchanged when they met on that day. Their common manhood had lost a kinsman."

Lowell's prose like his verse was enriched from the soil of many lands, but more and more as he grew older he wore his learning lightly. The self-consciousness of the young professor, ever anxious not to be tripped by the impertinence of some recalcitrant student, gave way toward the end to the easy discourse of a man sure of his ground. A certain tendency to superficial cleverness,—the stinging ironies of a yawning professor with a dull class flash out of his pages disagreeably at times, in odd contrast with his true and always delightful humor. Style must proceed from something solider than mere cleverness. Your tour de force performer is lucky to be remembered in a book of quotations; his definitive edition goes to the back shelf of the second-hand shop. Language with Lowell was a ready and flexible instrument. I have said that he knew men and books; he knew nature also, and he observed the passing pageant of his New England seasons with a shrewd and contemplative eye. The spring sunshine touching the old historic trees at Elmwood; the flashing gold of the oriole, the spendthrift glory of June days,—these things communicated an imperishable sunniness and charm to his writings. How happily, in one of the best of his papers—the essay on Walton—he has constructed for us the character of the delightful old angler. Walton, he darkly hints, is not the artless old customer we have always believed him; and you may be sure that only a lover of letters and a believer in style for the style's sake would chuckle—as we find Lowell doing,—at seeing the angler hesitating between two or three forms of a sentence, solicitous to preserve only the best. In his charming life of Herbert, after quoting a poem of Donne's, Walton adds a few words of characteristic comment. They wear a naïve air; they seem to have slipped carelessly from the pen. Walton wrote: "These hymns are now lost to us, but doubtless they were such as they two now sing in Heaven." "Now"—continues Lowell—"on the inside cover of his Eusebius, Walton has written three attempts at this sentence, each of them very far from the concise beauty to which he at last constrained himself. Simplicity, when it is not a careless gift of the Muse, is the last and most painful achievement of conscientious self-denial."

By the usual tests of style we might easily deal harshly with Emerson; but nothing could be idler than any attempt to buckram ourselves in the rules of the schoolroom in studying the qualities that make for style. Emerson's diction was happily adapted to the needs of his matter. His essays are like the headings for homely lectures or jottings from notebooks, and are almost as good reading when taken backward as forward, so little was he concerned with sequence or climax.

The roaring, steaming style of his grim old friend Carlyle never wakened any desire for emulation in the sage of Concord. Carlyle drives or drags you under the hot sun of mid-day, and if you falter or stumble he lays on the lash with a hard, bony Scotch hand. He was what Sydney Smith called Daniel Webster—a steam engine in trousers; but Emerson addresses you with a fine air of casualty when he meets you in the highway; and if the day be fine, and if you are in the mood for loitering, he will repeat to you the Socratic memoranda from his notebook. He is benignant, sanguine, wise, albeit a trifle cold with the chill of winter's last fling at the New England landscape. His usual essay reminds me of a string of icicles on the eaves of a white, staring New England house, aglitter but not yet adrip in the March sun. He is as careless of your attention as Walt Whitman when the good gray poet copies the names of "these states" from a geographical index. In spite of his fondness for references to the ancients he suggests Plato and Socrates far less than Poor Richard or Abe Martin. He contrived no new philosophy but he was a master-hand at labeling guideposts on the dusty highway of life. He could not build a bridge to carry us across the stream, but he could paint a sign—"no thoroughfare" or "A fine of ten dollars for driving faster than a walk": and happy is the youth who heeds these amiable warnings. Proverbs fell as naturally to his pen as codfish balls to his Sunday morning breakfast. He is as wholesome as whole wheat bread; but he has a frugal method with the bread-knife and the slices at his table are thin.

The more genial Lowell produces a cobwebbed bottle from his cellar and takes care to push it to your plate; he plies you with cakes spiced from far lands, and rises anon to kick the logs upon the hearth into leaping flame that the room may be fittingly dressed for cheering talk. Emerson patronizes you and advises a sparing draught from the austere-lipped pitcher of icy spring water. At seventeen (I give you my personal experience for what it may be worth), there is something tonic in the very austerity of his style,—his far-flung pickets that guard the frosty hills. Later on, when the fires of youth have cooled somewhat, and we march beside the veterans in the grand army;—when proverbs have lost their potency and the haversacks hang empty on our lean and weary backs, we prefer, for the campfires, authors of more red blood, and pass our battered cups for literary applejack that is none the worse for us if it tear our throats a little as it gurgles down. Once he might throw up his windows and call to us: Virtue is the soul's best aim; adjust your lives to truth; and so on. But now that we have tasted

battle and known shipwreck, we present arms only to
the hardier adjutants of the army of life who gallop by
on worn chargers and cry: "Courage, Comrade, the
devil's dead."

Eloquence of the truest and finest sort we find in
Ruskin at his happiest. He could be as wayward and
as provoking as Carlyle; but he founded a great ap-
ostolic line of teachers of beauty, and when he was
most abusive he was at least interesting, and when he
was possessed, as so often happened, by the spirit of
lovely things, and color and form and light wove their
spell for him and he wrought in an abandon of ecsta-
sy, we are aware of eloquence in its truest sense and
see style rising to its noblest possibilities. His tremendous earnestness, his zeal, his pictorial phraseology,
the glow of language struck off at heat,—these are
things that move us greatly in Ruskin. In his armory
he assembled a variety of weapons suitable for vari-
ous uses; he could administer mild rebuke; he could
expostulate a little stridently; he could deliver us up
to prison and slam the door of a mediæval dungeon
upon us; whereas the sour old Scot used one bloody
bludgeon for all heads. Carlyle was, to be sure, ca-
pable of tenderness—there were, indeed, few feats
possible in the literary gymnasium that he could not
accomplish; but when Jeannie got on his nerves there
was something doing in the Recording Angel's office.
Keble, he declared, was an ape, and Newman was
without the brains of a rabbit. He praised as violently

as he denounced;—everything was pitched in thundering hyperbole. The great men of the ages slunk through Carlyle's study like frightened steers through a slaughter house. Where he hid his own iniquities during his life time the genial Froude exposed them in a new chamber of horrors at his death.

Macaulay always reminds me of a gentleman whip driving a coach and four. He manages his horses with a sure hand. His speed is never too high; he knows the smooth roads and rumbles along at a comfortable gallop, swinging up to tavern doors with grand climaxes. He writes as a man writes who dines well and feels good; he piles up a few pages of manuscript after the supper gong has sounded just to show that his head is still full after his stomach is empty. He can turn his horses in the chancel of a cathedral without knocking out a single choir stall; he can drive under low arches without ruffling his hat; his knowledge of the road is complete; his confidence reassuring. As you roll over the road with the whip lash curling and cracking and the horn blowing blithely you submit yourself to his guidance with supreme faith that he will never spill you into the ditch or send you crashing into a fence corner. English history unfolds before him like a charming panorama. We smile but are not convinced by that reference of Dr. Holmes to the Macaulay flowers of literature. You are proud of yourself to be reading anything so wholly agreeable and apparently so wise. The later scientific method of historical writing can not harden our hearts toward Macaulay. A man whose pen never scratched or squeaked is not to be set aside for a spectacled professor in a moldy library. His facts may be misleading but—he's perfectly bully reading!

It is difficult to speak of Stevenson, for he has been so much cited, and his admirers praise him with so much exuberance that many are on guard against what is called his charm. He has undoubtedly been praised by some who liked his velvet coat better than his writings; and yet when we have dismissed these triflers and have locked away the velvet jacket we must admit that the applause of the tavern idlers is not without reason. We have to do now only with his style,—the style that is indubitably there. It not only exists, but there is an eerie, luring, Ariel-like quality about it that can not readily be shaken off. He has told us with a frankness rarely equaled by men of letters of the methods he employed in learning to write: his confessions have been quoted ad nauseam,—I refer to those paragraphs in which he tells us how he played the sedulous ape to many accepted masters of style in the hope of catching their tricks.

The gods of his youth were certainly respectable,—Hazlitt, Lamb, Wordsworth, Sir Thomas Browne, Defoe, Hawthorne, Montaigne and Obermann. He not only confesses that he aped these models; he defends the method: "Nor yet," he says, "if you are born original, is there anything in this training that shall clip the wings of your originality."

Stevenson liked a good phrase just as he liked a good inn, or winter stars or a long white road. A zest for life,—for the day's adventure, for the possibilities of the next turn of the highway, for a pungent saying that might fall from the lips of a passing beggar,—such things as these interested him, and he accommodated his style to the business of setting them forth in melodious language. He realized in a fine way that which we heavily call the light touch,—a touch firm in its lightness and instinct with nimbleness and grace. We should know from his writings, if he had not been described with so much particularity, that he was a person of keen humor and delightful vivacity. Everything that may be done with the light touch he did and did well. He renewed our interest in the essay; he wrote poems marked by a shy but bubbling joy in simple things; he mounted the fallen lord of romance upon a fresh charger and sent pirate caravels forth again to plunder the seas. And as he sails the wide waters of romance under flags not down in the signal books, we may be quite sure that every bit of brass is polished to the utmost, that every rope is in place and neatly coiled and every sail furled tightly in the nattiest manner or bent to catch the gale. Those cheerless souls who never heard a whip handle rattle a tavern shutter at midnight, who never prowled about old wharves and talked with tattooed sailormen; who are grim seekers after realities and have no eye for the light that never was on sea or land have no business with Stevenson and had better stick to tea, muffins and The Ladies' Home Journal. And finally—for we must hurry on lest we fall under that spell of his, let me say that the sense of form and the instinctive blending of word colors,—things of no light importance in consideration of style, have not in our time been better exemplified than in the writings of Stevenson.

You will observe that I have been calling the roll of names near to our own generation, for these we may bring to a more intimate scrutiny; and I am not among those who are confident that the last word was said in English style before the Victorian era. The nervous energy of our later English comes naturally with the quicker currents of life. Milton, himself, if he might reappear from the shadows, would be sure to delatinize his speech, and accommodate his manner, in all likelihood, to the requirements of less monstrous subjects than those offered by the decadent years in English history which saw the blackguard roundheads sticking their bloody spears through cathedral windows.

The style of Mr. Henry James is much discussed, frequently execrated and often deplored; and even in a hasty glance like ours over the bookshelves we must linger a moment beside his long line of volumes.

Whether we admire or dislike him he is not a negligible figure in contemporaneous literature. He is one of the most interesting writers of his time; he has uttered himself with remarkable fullness; he has attempted and succeeded in many things. His influence upon younger writers has been very great. Mr. Owen Wister has lately acknowledged his own indebtedness; Mrs. Wharton's obligations are written large on all her pages. Mr. James is, to use a word of his own, immensely provocative. The range of his interest is wide and his cultivation in certain directions great. He is not a scholar in the sense that Lowell was; he has observed life in shorter perspectives; his literary criticisms, which we may take to be a key to his personal interests, have dealt with nearer figures,—with Tourguenief, Balzac and Stevenson. His paper on Stevenson remains and will long remain the most admirable and the most searching thing written on the lad in the velvet jacket. Herein we find an instructive and illuminative denotement of Mr. James' own attitude toward this trade of writing; every writer, he declares, who respects himself and his art cares greatly for his phrase; but Stevenson, he finds, cares more for life. Mr. James is no scorner of phrase for the phrase's sake or of form for form's sake. The essays collected in "Partial Portraits" and "English Hours" are written in a far directer and simpler manner than his later tales. There are few lean streaks in Mr. James' writings. He sees through and all around the things he writes about, whether it be a city, a bit of landscape, a character of fiction, or an author. When a subject takes hold of him the aroused thoughts tumble about in tumultuous fashion; he is not a little cistern easily emptied but a great flowing well. Most of us complain that in later years he has been inarticulate, or obscure, and often utterly incomprehensible. There is some justice in the charge, and it can not be pretended that "The Golden Bowl" or the essays he has recently printed on American cities are easy reading. The style of these later writings is radically different from that of "Washington Square," "Roderick Hudson" and "The Portrait of a Lady." But the difficulties of this later manner may be accounted for, I believe, on the theory that his own amazing abundance throws his powers of expression into confusion. We must admit that Mr. James often stammers, sputters and sticks. His creative vision is so wide that his expression is often unequal to representing it in the familiar symbols of speech. It is at moments of this sort that he leaves us to stumble in a dark stair-case; then suddenly we are aware of his leading hand again, urging us on, and down the hall a brilliant light flashes forth, and we are able to see things again with his eyes as his expression once more catches step with his ideas. His power of phrase is very great indeed. Certainly no other American writer equals him in the knack of flinging into a few words some positively illuminating idea. A phrase with him has often the brilliancy of the spot light in the theater, that falls unexpectedly upon the face of a concealed player and holds for a moment the attention of the spectators. I take up without previous examination a paper on the City of Washington in "The American Scene" and read this passage: "Hereabouts," he writes, "beyond doubt, history had from of old seemed to me insistently seated, and I remember a short springtime of years ago when Lafayette Square itself, contiguous to the Executive Mansion, could create a rich sense of the past by the use of scarce other witchcraft than its command of that pleasant perspective, and its possession of the most prodigious of all Presidential effigies, Andrew Jackson, as archaic as a Ninevite king, prancing and rocking through the ages."

He seems, in this later manner which has been so much discussed, to have lost his contact with the old familiar symbols of feeling and sense and to have resolved the world into a place of sublimated abstractions, which he describes sometimes with a stammering and inadequate tongue and again in bursts of rugged eloquence and with amazing penetration. The smoothness of the ordered thought, the pretty balances, the march and swing of the old cadences of our speech are either beyond him or beneath him, and in a man of so acute and full a mind and with a sophistication so complete in all that makes for beauty, we can not do less than subscribe to the theory that he knows what he is about and that his style, in the curious phase to which he has brought it, is a true expression of the oddly oblique lines and strangely concentric circles of his matured mind.

Eloquence is, I have sometimes thought, the rarest quality that may be embraced in the essentials of style. We need not quibble over definitions. "Eloquence," said Dean Farrar, "is the noble, the harmonious, the passionate expression of truths profoundly realized, or of emotions intensely felt"; and it is sufficient for our purposes. The term is applied commonly and uncritically in oratory. I have not myself found the reading of the speeches of great orators profitable, charmed they never so marvelously in their own day. The old school readers served us well in this particular by their admirable selections.

Judgments of the ear and of the eye vary widely. The sentences that read well will as likely as not fall flat when spoken, even when uttered with force. The oration delivered on the field of Gettysburg by Edward Everett is commonly spoken of in contemptuous contrast with Lincoln's utterance on the same occasion, but there can be no fair comparison between the two performances. Everett was indisputably one of the greatest forensic orators of his time,—scholarly, elegant, impressive. What Lincoln wrote and read at Gettysburg was not an oration but—to use Carl Schurz's happy characterization of it—a sonorous and beautiful psalm. The familiar story that Lincoln began and finished that address on the train between Washington and Gettysburg was denied by Mr. John

G. Nicolay, who has somewhere written a most interesting account of its preparation.

It is difficult to imagine a severer test of the mind's gift of expression than the extemporaneous speech, evoked by some emergency and spoken without premeditation. Such instances are indeed rare, for your orator is, I find, something of a liar. He likes to give the impression of readiness of tongue and wit; whereas the speech he has flung off at some crisis of a debate, seemingly produced on his feet, may have been carried in his mind for weeks.

We Americans have long been accustomed to florid style of public address. I remember hearing it said often in my youth that the newspaper was driving out the orator, but I do not believe that this is true, or that it will ever be true. The glow and passion of the spoken word must always hold a fascination for men that is not possible in the printed appeal. The general rise of popular intelligence raises the standard somewhat; mere bombast and spread-eagleism—the nimble ascent to pyramidal climaxes,—is less effective as the years go by; but the spell-binder has not yet been superseded. He may not always convince, but he dare not be dull, and he now and then rises to the level of a Benjamin Harrison, who combined the cogent reasoning of the deeply philosophical lawyer with a rare art in marshaling his facts, and addressed himself to the conscience and the reason of his audiences.

Terror and horror are rarely evoked by our later orators. Even the slaughter of the innocents in the Philippines in the amiable Christian effort to extend our beneficent empire to Asia has brought forth no really striking protest worthy of the cause. In the same senate chamber where the hired counsel of the railways and other trust-protecting and subsidy-hunting felons subsequently thwarted the will of the American people, Thomas Corwin, a senator in congress from Ohio, on the 11th of February, 1847, thus delivered himself on the continuation of the war with Mexico. I quote this paragraph from Senator Corwin's speech in reply to Senator Cass of Michigan merely to illustrate the possibilities of passionate oratory skillfully employed:

"Sir, look at this picture of want of room! With twenty millions of people, you have about one thousand millions of acres of land, inviting settlement by every conceivable argument, bringing them down to a quarter of a dollar an acre and allowing every man to squat where he pleases. But the Senator from Michigan says we will be two hundred millions in a few years and we want room. If I were a Mexican I would tell you, 'Have you not room in your own country to bury your dead men? If you come into mine we will greet you with bloody hands and welcome you to hospitable graves.'"

And while we are touching upon the literary style of statesmen you will pardon me for quoting further, in illustration of the reluctance, caution and restraint that may check the exuberance of personal feeling, from a statement made by Colonel Theodore Roosevelt in January, 1904: He said:

"In John Hay I have a great Secretary of State. In Philander Knox I have a great Attorney-General. In other Cabinet posts I have great men. Elihu Root could take any of these places and fill it as well as the man who is now there. And, in addition, he is what probably none of these gentlemen could be, a great Secretary of War. Elihu Root is the ablest man I have known in our Government service. I will go further. He is the greatest man that has appeared in the public life of any country, in any position, on either side of the ocean, in my time."

Criticism offers no adequately descriptive word for this type of reserved, unventurous statement. Let us consider whether it may not properly be styled the imperial theodoric.

Now, in conclusion,—if such disjecta membra as these may have a conclusion—we have only skirted the nearer coasts; what you have heard has been the merest memorandum of a somewhat haphazard voyage. No hour's excursion can carry us far in our quest of the secret of style.

If the wide sea of literature could be charted, then we all might find the ports into which the master mariners have sailed their crafts; but we labor with a broken oar and our log book is a tame record of vain attempts to land on impossible shores. We see many great ships hull down on the horizon, but dare not follow them far;—the majestic caravel of George Meredith bearing ingots of pure gold, as rough and clean as Browning lyrics; and close beside it the stately craft of George Eliot,—would that there were time to go aboard and wrest their secrets from them! And I must not omit that rarely gifted English woman, Mrs. Alice Meynell. Her prose happily expresses the delicacy and grace of an imagination whose province lies beyond the Ivory Portal of the Realm of Dreams.

Turning inland we see deploying upon a glittering plain an army with banners, preceded by a mitered host chanting in deep Gregorian. Entre per me! shouts a charging knight galloping forward with a great clatter of arms and armor. We recognize one of Maurice Hewlett's many inventions. Hewlett manages an archaic manner admirably; a trifle over-elaborate maybe, but there is muscle beneath the embroidery. Afar off steams the battleship Rudyard Kipling, and we know the young Admiral for a man of high courage, at home on land or sea, in the air above or in the waters under the earth. And if we may pause for one word, we may say that the tremendous importance, the hardly calculable influence of the English Bible

on English style has nowhere in our generation been better evidenced than in the writings of Kipling. Not merely that he so often quotes from the Bible; not so much that biblical phrases abound in his pages; but that the directness, the simplicity, the rugged power of Hebrew narrative imparts a singular distinction and force to all he writes. Young writers, intent upon the best possibilities of our mother English, do well to leave all that the great Greeks, the great Latins, the great Italians and French have written until they have wrought,—into the very alphabet of memory,—the innumerable lessons and high examples of that imperishable text book of English style.

Ah, if it were a mere pagan chronicle; if it were the least spiritual book in the world, still we who love English literature must go to it, as one who thirsteth, to a familiar and well-loved spring, longing for it verily as "David longed, and said, oh, that one would give me drink of the water of the well of Bethlehem, that is by the gate!"